Friday Afternoon Fun

Story by Julie Ellis

Illustrations by Naomi C. Lewis

Contents

Chapter 1

The Running Race

Emma and Matthew looked over
at the parents who were standing
by the running track.
They saw their mother waving to them.

"Hi, Mum," called Emma. "I'm glad you came."

"I'm going to win this race!" shouted Matthew.

Everyone in the class got ready
for the first race.

"Catch me if you can," Matthew said to Emma.
He knew that he was the fastest runner
in the class.

"Ready... **go!**" called the teacher.

The children ran down the track
as fast as they could.

Soon Matthew was in front.

Emma tried very hard.
She ran past three children.
Now the only one in front of her was Matthew.

Matthew looked back.
He was surprised to see Emma
so close behind him.

Emma kept looking ahead,
and she ran past Matthew
just as they got to the finishing line.

6

"Good running," said Mum, giving them a hug.

Emma was very happy,
but Matthew was not pleased with himself.

Chapter 2

The Egg and Spoon Race

"It's the egg and spoon race, now," said Emma.
"You could win this one, Matthew."

"I'm not going in any more races today,"
said Matthew.

"Races are not about being first," said Mum.
"They are about having a go and having fun."

"Come on, Matthew," said Emma.
"The egg and spoon race will be fun."

"All right," he said. "I'll have a go.
I might beat you this time."

The children lined up.

"Ready. . . **go**!" called the teacher.

Matthew walked fast,
but he was very careful.
He kept watching the egg on his spoon.

Emma tried to run past him.
But the egg on her spoon started to wobble,
and it fell off.

"Well done, Matthew," said Mum,
as he crossed the line first.
"I'm proud of you for having a go."

Chapter 3

The Sack Race

Just then, the teacher called out,
"It's time for the parents' race."

"Go on, Mum," said Emma.

"No," said Mum.
"I can't run fast like you two."

"You can do it, Mum!" said Emma.
"You might win because this is a sack race."

"Races are not about always being first,"
said Matthew, with a big smile.
"They are about having a go and having fun."

Mum laughed. "All right," she said.
"I'll have a go."

"Go, Mum!" shouted Matthew and Emma.

Mum tried hard, but she fell over
because she was laughing so much.

"Don't worry, Mum!" said Matthew.
"We're proud of you!"